DISNEP · PIXAR

TOY STORY

The Junior Novelization

Adapted by Cathy East Dubowski
Based on the screenplay by
Joss Whedon, Andrew Stanton,
Joel Cohen, and Alec Sokolow

Random House 🏠 **New York**

Chapter

In the bedroom of young Andy Davis, a desperate outlaw was about to be captured.

As a group of toys gathered in a quiet western town—made out of a row of cardboard boxes—the outlaw suddenly appeared.

"All right, everyone, this is a stickup!" said Andy in a gruff voice, pretending to be a villainous Mr. Potato Head. "Don't anybody move!"

All the other toys were carefully placed in position, watching. Andy pretended to make them all talk.

Andy picked up his piggy bank and shook out its coins. He lowered Mr. Potato Head over the money greedily. Then Andy grabbed a porcelain Little Bo Peep figurine. "Stop it, you mean old potato!" he said in a high-pitched voice, pretending to be Bo Peep.

"Quiet, Bo Peep, or your sheep get run over!" growled Mr. Potato Head. In the middle of a toy racetrack, the sheep stood helplessly, right in the path of danger.

"Not my sheep! Somebody do something!" Bo Peep cried.

Suddenly, Andy grabbed a brown-haired cowboy sheriff doll named Woody. He yanked on the shiny white plastic ring that dangled from a string on the toy sheriff's back. A small voice box inside the cowboy's chest squawked a scratchy recorded message: *"Reach for the sky!"*

"I'm here to stop you," Woody said to Mr. Potato Head. "Are you gonna come quietly?"

"You can't touch me, Sheriff!" Mr. Potato Head shouted. "I brought my attack dog with a built-in force field!"

Andy stretched a toy Slinky dog in front of Mr. Potato Head, then grabbed a plastic Tyrannosaurus rex doll and dropped it on top of Slinky.

"Well, I brought my dinosaur, who eats force-field dogs! You're goin' to jail," declared Sheriff Woody.

Andy's baby sister, Molly, watched from behind the bars of her crib. Taped to one side of the crib was a cardboard sign with the word JAIL scrawled in crayon.

Andy dropped Mr. Potato Head in with Molly. With a shrieking giggle, the little girl grabbed the doll and started banging him against the rail of her crib, knocking some of his parts onto the floor.

"You saved the day again, Woody," Andy said as he pulled the sheriff's string once more.

"*You're my favorite deputy,*" Woody replied.

Andy galloped into the hall. He propped Woody on the stairwell railing—and shoved. Whooping and hollering, Andy clattered downstairs as Woody slid awkwardly down the banister.

"Gotcha!" Andy cried at the bottom. He put Woody on his shoulder and romped around the living room. Then he placed the doll on the footrest of a recliner chair, pulled the lever, and catapulted him across the room.

Suddenly, Andy's eyes lit up. He ran toward his mother, leaving Woody sprawled on the couch. "Wow! This looks great, Mom!"

Colorful helium balloons bobbed on their strings. Crepe-paper streamers decorated the dining room walls. A banner draped across the archway read: HAPPY BIRTHDAY, ANDY!

"Can we leave this up till we move?" Andy asked his mother.

"Well, sure, we can leave it up," replied Mrs. Davis. "Now, go get Molly. Your friends are going to be here any minute."

Andy stopped by the couch to pick up Woody. "It's party time, Woody!"

Andy pounded up the stairs to his room. As he propped Woody on the bed, he pulled the toy sheriff's string one last time.

"*Somebody's poisoned the water hole*," said Woody.

"Come on, Molly." Andy reached into his sister's "jail" and lifted her out. Without looking back, he called over his shoulder, "See ya later, Woody!"

Slam! Andy kicked the door closed behind him. The room was silent for a moment. Then Woody shoved his hat back and scratched his forehead. A worried frown creased his brow as he sat up.

"Pull my string!" he muttered under his breath. "The birthday party's today?"

Woody knew only too well what birthdays meant: toys. New toys, and lots of them. Shiny. Still nice in their boxes, with all their parts. Clean, and full of promise. Woody glanced around the quiet room.

"Okay, everybody," he called out. "Coast is clear!"

Slowly, toys began to roll out from under the bed, toddle across the floor, and bounce out of the toy chest. They flip-flopped down from shelves. Chattering, squeaking, quacking, and ringing, they swarmed into the open terrain of the bedroom floor.

Mr. Potato Head wobbled as he sat up on his rounded bottom. He had a blank expression, since all his face parts were strewn around the room. One by one, he jabbed his plastic eyes, ears, nose, and mouth into the small round holes scattered across his body. Then he walked over to Andy's fat pink piggy bank, who was flipping a penny into his coin slot. "Hey, look, Hamm! I'm Picasso!"

The piggy bank stared at Mr. Potato Head, whose face pieces were stuck into the wrong holes, making his features seem all mixed up, as in one of the famous artist's paintings. Hamm blinked. "I don't get it."

"Ah, you uncultured swine!" Mr. Potato Head sighed in disgust as he put his features back where they belonged.

High atop Andy's mattress, Woody turned to a plastic Green Army Man standing guard on the bedside table. "Hey, Sarge. Have you seen Slinky?"

"No, sir!" the sergeant said with a stiff salute.

"Okay, thank you. At ease." Woody leaped off the bed, the spurs of his brown boots jangling when he landed squarely on the floor. "Hey, Slinky?"

A metal *fwump!* sounded under the bed. Two paws shoved a checkerboard out from under the hem of the bedspread. Woody's faithful sidekick, the toy Slinky dog, wandered out and began setting up the checkers.

"I'm red this time," Slinky said.

Woody shook his head. "No, Slink."

"Oh, all right. You can be red if you want."

"Not now, Slink!" Woody shook his head again. "I've got some bad news."

"Bad news?" Slinky yelped.

Woody shoved a hand over Slinky's mouth and looked around. A few nearby toys inclined their heads, listening for any scrap of hot gossip. Woody led Slinky a few steps away.

"Just gather everyone up for a staff meeting—and be happy!" he whispered.

"Got it," said Slinky. He forced a quick laugh, then shuffled off across the room.

Woody heard a floor-sweeping swish and glanced down at a toy snake and a shiny toy robot as he walked toward the end of the bed.

"Staff meeting, everybody," Woody said, then added, "Snake, Robot—podium duty."

The snake and the robot grumbled a little, but they crawled out from under the bed to help.

A few paces away, the sheriff heard a squeak. He grinned. The knobs were twitching on Etch A Sketch, Andy's rectangular drawing toy. "Hey, Etch!" the sheriff called out. "Draw!"

Woody's gun arm shot to his empty holster. Too late.

Etch A Sketch had beaten him to the draw. Etch proudly displayed the revolver he'd created on his gray screen.

"You got me again, Etch!" Woody teased. "You've been working on that draw. Fastest knobs in the West!" Woody patted him on the corner of his red plastic frame, then walked toward the podium, which the snake and the robot were building out of some blocks and a Tinker Toy box.

Woody nodded his approval. The meeting would start soon. He'd better make a list.

"Now, where is that— Hey, who moved my doodle pad way over here?" He walked over and picked up the tablet.

Suddenly, behind him—

"*Roaaaarrrr!*"

Woody casually turned around. "Oh, how ya doin', Rex?"

Rex, the not-very-ferocious-looking plastic tyrannosaur, smiled hopefully, his tiny claws clutched to his chest. "Were you scared? Tell me honestly."

Woody bit his lip and cleared his throat. "I was close to being scared that time."

Rex sighed and followed Woody toward the podium. "I'm going for fearsome here," he explained. "But I just don't feel it. I think I'm just coming off as annoying."

Woody was about to reply, but a shepherd's crook suddenly hooked him around the neck. One big yank and he found himself nose to nose with a smiling Bo Peep. "Oh . . . hi, Bo."

The slender figurine batted her blue eyes. "I wanted to thank you, Woody," she said. "For saving my flock."

Woody blushed. "Oh, hey—it was nothing."

Bo Peep smiled sweetly. "What do you say I get someone else to watch the sheep tonight?" she purred. Woody gulped.

Bo gestured with her crook toward the alphabet blocks that decorated the base of her lamp. "Remember," she added, "I'm just a couple of blocks away." With a little wave, she sashayed past a small pile of toy alphabet blocks and headed toward the podium.

Woody's heart *boing*ed like a jack-in-the-box. He shook his head to clear it and glanced around. All business again, he scribbled some notes on his doodle pad and strode toward the podium.

Slinky was busy herding all the toys into place. "Come on, come on! Smaller toys up front!"

Everyone crowded around expectantly as Woody took his place at the podium. A toy tape recorder waddled up beside him.

"Oh, thanks, Mike," Woody said. He picked up Mike's microphone and blew. "Hello? Testing, testing. Everybody hear me? Great."

He glanced down at the notes on his doodle pad.

"Okay. First item today: Has everyone picked a moving buddy?"

All the toys began talking excitedly.

"I didn't know we were supposed to have one already," Rex whined.

Mr. Potato Head held up one of his extra plastic arms. "Do we have to hold hands?"

The toys nudged one another and laughed. Woody shook his head. "Oh, yeah. You guys think this is a big joke. We've only got one week left before the move. I don't want any toys left behind. A moving buddy—if you don't have one, get one!"

Woody looked back at his doodle pad. "All right, next. . . . Oh, yes. Tuesday night's Plastic Corrosion Awareness meeting was a big success, and we want to thank Mr. Spell for putting that on for us. Thanks, Mr. Spell."

"You're welcome," the electronic Mr. Spell droned, the words scrolling across his display screen.

Woody stared at his list, stalling. There was no use putting it off any longer. He had bad news. The toys would have to be told.

"Oh, yes. One minor note here." Woody's voice dropped to a whisper. "Andy's birthday party's been moved to today." He coughed and shouted, "Next, we have—"

The room exploded into squeaks, squeals, bells, barks, and whistles.

"What do you mean, the party's today?" Rex

exclaimed. "His birthday's not till next week!"

Woody held up his hands. "Well, obviously Andy's mom wanted to have the party before the move. I'm not worried. You shouldn't be worried."

Mr. Potato Head elbowed his way to the front of the crowd, glaring at the sheriff. "Of course Woody ain't worried!" he cried. "He's been Andy's favorite since kindergarten!"

Some of the toys mumbled their agreement.

"Hey! Come on, Potato Head," Slinky responded, speaking up for his pal. "If Woody says it's all right, then, well, darn it, it's good enough for me. Woody has never steered us wrong before."

Woody jumped down from the podium and walked through the crowd, looking each toy straight in the eye. "Listen, no one's getting re-placed," he said soothingly. "It doesn't matter how much we're played with. What matters is that we're here for Andy when he needs us. That's what we're made for. Right?"

One by one, the whirring, muttering, chiming toys fell silent, feeling at least a little reassured.

Hamm the piggy bank finally broke the silence. "Pardon me," he called from the windowsill. "I hate to break up the staff meeting, but . . . THEY'RE HERE! BIRTHDAY GUESTS AT THREE O'CLOCK!"

Chapter

The peaceful bedroom erupted into chaos. Woody held up his hands. "Stay calm, everyone!" he shouted with authority.

CRUNCH!

Too late. Like a herd of stampeding cattle, the toys bolted over Woody toward the bedroom window. Even Mike yanked his microphone out of Woody's hand and hopped away.

Woody reeled, staring as the crowd rushed off. Then he shrugged and announced, "Uh, meeting adjourned." No one heard him. They were already plastered to the windowpane.

Hamm gulped as he gazed through the window, down into the front yard. "Oh, boy. Will ya take a look at all those presents?"

"I can't see a thing!" Mr. Potato Head complained. He pulled his eyes out of his head and held them above the crowd, aimed out the window.

He and the other toys stared in horror. On the street below, kids sprang from their parents' cars, each carrying an object that struck fear into the hearts of Andy's toys.

Birthday presents.

Hamm shook his head. "Yessir, we're next month's garage sale fodder for sure."

"Any dinosaur-shaped ones?" Rex asked worriedly.

"Ah, for crying out loud," Hamm jeered. "They're all in boxes!"

Rex said nervously, "They're getting bigger!"

"Wait!" said Slinky. "There's a nice little one over there."

He pointed at a boy who was facing away from the window. Only the tiny tip of a present showed. Then the boy turned. The present was more than four feet long!

"AAAAAHHHH!" screamed the toys.

"We're doomed!" Rex howled.

The toys began to wail and moan. Woody sighed. Things were getting way out of control. He had to do something fast, or he'd have a serious problem on his hands. "All right! All right!" he called out.

The toys turned and faced Woody. Never had he seen them look so frightened. He sighed and smiled affectionately at his friends. "If I send out the troops, will you all calm down?"

"Yes! Yes! We promise!" Rex cried.

Woody strode briskly toward the nightstand. "Sergeant!" he shouted up to the tabletop. "Establish a recon post downstairs. Code Red. You know what to do."

"Yes, SIR!" the little Green Army Man replied. He shinnied down a leg of the nightstand, then dashed to the corner, where a plastic container labeled BUCKET O' SOLDIERS stood.

Sarge shouted, and a platoon of green soldiers peeked out of the top of the bucket. "All right, men!" he barked. "You heard him. Code Red. Repeat: We are at Code Red!" He waved the group forward. "Let's move, move, move!"

One by one, the plastic soldiers jumped out of their bucket barracks and marched double-time in a line toward the door.

Creeeeaak . . . Andy's bedroom door eased open. A single Green Army scout crept into the upstairs hall, scoping for any signs of danger.

Satisfied that the coast was clear, the scout signaled to the other troops. Dozens of soldiers streamed forward, carefully transporting the specialized equipment they needed for their intelligence mission: a jump rope and a baby monitor.

The soldiers darted behind the banister and held their position. Sarge surveyed their route through binoculars.

Paratroopers crept to the edge of the landing, then bravely leaped off. *Fwump!* Their parachutes opened, carrying them safely to the polished wood floor below.

After a quick look around, they signaled to the soldiers who were waiting above. All clear! Seconds later, more soldiers slid down, using Andy's jump rope.

The troops marched toward the living room. Suddenly, a door opened. They heard footsteps. They froze in position. As Mrs. Davis came through the door, her shoe stomped down in the middle of the squad.

"What in the world?" She frowned at the toy army men scattered across the floor and shook her head. With Andy's party in full swing, she was too busy to stop and pick up toys. Using the toe of her shoe, she simply kicked the army men out of the way.

As soon as she was gone, Sarge motioned to the handful of men still waiting above on the stairs. Carefully they came down the jump rope, riding the baby monitor, which was tied securely and lowered to the floor. When everyone reached the ground, the soldiers quickly dragged the monitor toward a potted plant.

Sarge started to follow but noticed that one of his men had been injured. Holding his leg, the soldier waved for his commander to keep moving. "Go on without me!"

But Sarge would have none of that. "A good soldier never leaves a man behind," he said as he helped the injured soldier to his feet.

Suddenly, Sarge put a finger to his lips and cocked his head. More footsteps—lots of them. And they were coming this way!

Sarge dragged the injured soldier toward the living room. The two army men stumbled to safety behind the potted plant just as the first pair of feet stomped past.

The crew quickly set up the baby monitor. Sarge scanned the horizon with his binoculars. He spotted his target.

On the Davises' living room coffee table, a tower of gift-wrapped packages loomed toward the ceiling. Sarge whistled softly through his teeth, then leaned into the baby monitor.

"Come in, Mother Bird. This is Alpha Bravo."

Upstairs in Andy's room, Woody and his friends clustered around the receiver. "This is it!" Woody cried excitedly. "Quiet, quiet, quiet!"

Sarge's deep voice came through loud and clear. *"Andy's opening the first present now."*

In the suspenseful silence, Mr. Potato Head crossed his fingers and chanted, "Mrs. Potato Head . . . Mrs. Potato Head . . ." Rex shot him a weird look.

"Hey, I can dream, can't I?" said Mr. Potato Head.

"The bow's coming off," Sarge's voice reported through the monitor. *"He's ripping the wrapping paper. . . . It's a . . . it's a . . ."* The toys held their breath.

"It's a lunch box!" Sarge announced. *"We've got a lunch box here!"* The toys clapped and cheered.

"*Okay,*" came Sarge's voice. "*Second present.*" The toys hushed and leaned forward expectantly.

"*It appears to be . . . Okay, it's bedsheets.*"

"Who invited *that* kid?" asked Mr. Potato Head. But again, Andy's toys were relieved.

One by one, Sarge reported on each present as Andy unwrapped it. Each time it was good news. Slowly, the toys began to relax a little.

"*Okay,*" Sarge said at last. "*We're on the last present now. It's a big one. . . .*" Every stuffed, plastic, and wooden head in Andy's room leaned forward.

"*It's a . . . It's a board game!*" Sarge revealed. "*Repeat: Battleship!*" All the toys let out cheers of relief. Battleship was a toy they could all live with.

"All right!" Hamm shouted. He pounded Mr. Potato Head on the back so hard that his face parts flew off.

"Hey, watch it!" said Mr. Potato Head.

"Sorry there, old Spudhead," replied Hamm.

"So, did I tell you? Huh? Nothing to worry about," Woody said.

Slinky yipped happily. "I knew you were right all along, Woody. Never doubted you for a second."

❆　❆　❆

Downstairs, Sarge congratulated his men. They began to pack up their equipment.

"Wait a minute!" The sound of Mrs. Davis's voice stopped Sarge in his tracks.

"Wait!" he whispered to his men.

Sarge watched, tense, as Mrs. Davis jumped up and hurried to the coat closet by the front door. She tossed a teasing look over her shoulder, then smiled. "Ooooh, what do we have here?"

"Turn that thing back on!" Sarge ordered, pointing at the baby monitor. A soldier rammed the switch.

"Come in, Mother Bird!" Sarge said frantically. *"Mom has pulled a surprise present from the closet. Andy's opening it. He's really excited! It's*

a huge package. Oh, one of the kids is in the way. I can't see."

At last, the kid moved out of the way. Sarge blinked. *"It's . . . it's a . . . "* Sarge and his soldiers gaped at the unwrapped present as the kids screamed in delight. It was worse than any of the toys could have imagined.

Upstairs, the rest of the toys waited, their hearts pounding. Rex grabbed a nightstand leg and shook it in frustration. "It's a what? What is it?"

Thwack! The monitor fell off the table and its batteries rolled across the floor. All the toys were shouting. Mr. Potato Head pounced on the batteries and tried to stick them back into the monitor.

"No, no! Turn 'em around!" Woody hollered.

"You're puttin' 'em in backwards!" Hamm cried.

Woody shoved Hamm and Mr. Potato Head aside. He grabbed a battery and jammed it in the right way. As soon as he snapped the second one in, Sarge's voice crackled urgently across the room:

"Red Alert! Andy is coming upstairs! Juvenile intrusion. Repeat: Resume your positions now!"

"Andy's coming!" Woody shouted. "Everybody—back to your places. Hurry!" The toys scattered.

"Where's my ear?" Mr. Potato Head cried, scrambling across the floor. "Did you see my ear?"

Splat! Rex smashed into a trash can as the sound of pounding footsteps came closer and closer. The door banged open. Woody fell limp in his special spot on the bed just as Andy and his friends charged in. The kids were all jabbering at once.

"Hey, look! Its lasers light up."

"Take that, Zurg!" Andy cried. Then a mob of kids pounced on Andy's bed. Woody felt himself being shoved out of the way. He slid off the side of the bed and fell to the floor. His heart sank.

"Quick! Make a space! This is where the spaceship lands."

Woody tried desperately to see what they were talking about. But there were too many kids in the way. Still, he was sure of one thing: A brand-new toy had arrived.

Chapter

Woody lay beneath the bed as he listened to Andy and his friends chatter.

"Look," Andy said. "You press his back and he does a karate-chop action."

"Come on down, guys!" Mrs. Davis called up the stairs. "It's time for games. We've got prizes!"

"Oh, yeah!" Andy said. He led his pack of noisy friends out of the room. The door slammed.

Slowly, cautiously, Andy's toys came to life. They crept toward the bed, where Andy had left his new toy.

"What is it?"

"Can you see it?"

"Woody?" Rex whispered. "Who's up there with you?"

Coughing from the dust, Woody crawled out from under the bed. The toys gasped in shock.

"Woody!" Slinky exclaimed. "What are you doing under the bed?"

Woody pulled himself to his feet and slapped the dust from his jeans.

"Uh . . . nothing! I'm sure Andy was just a little excited, that's all. Too much cake and ice cream, I suppose. It's just a mistake."

"Well," said Mr. Potato Head, "that 'mistake' is sitting in your spot, Woody."

Rex gasped. "Have you been replaced?"

Woody put one hand on his hip and spoke firmly. "Hey! What did I tell you earlier? No one is getting replaced." But the other toys weren't so sure.

"Now," Woody continued, "let's all be polite and give whatever it is up there a nice big Andy's room welcome."

Woody smiled confidently, ignoring the butterflies in the pit of his stomach. He turned and clambered back up the side of the bed.

As Woody peered over the top of the bed, late-afternoon sunlight streamed in through the window, momentarily blinding him. He blinked and began to make out a dark silhouette standing tall against the light. And then he could see.

A toy man—unlike any Woody had ever encountered—stood boldly in the center of Andy's bed. He wore a white high-tech space suit. A green control panel studded with a complex array of push buttons, stickers, and lights covered the top half of his broad chest. A clear plastic bubble shielded his head. Through this helmet, Woody could see the arched brow, keen eyes, and strong chin of a confident explorer.

As Woody gawked, the stranger came to life and pressed a blue button on the right side of his chest. *Bleep! Bleep!*

"Buzz Lightyear to Star Command. Come in, Star Command." The figure paused for an answer. No response.

"Star Command," he repeated more forcefully. "Do you read me?" His mouth tightened into a stiff grimace. "Why don't they answer?" He took a step; then something caught his eye.

Woody followed the new toy's gaze. Buzz was staring at the smashed box in which he had been packaged. The space figure gasped.

"My ship!" he cried. He ran to the crumpled box to examine the damage. "Blast! This'll take weeks to repair!"

Fuming, he flipped open a plastic compartment strapped to his arm. "Buzz Lightyear Mission Log. Star date four-zero-seven-two: My ship has run off course en route to Sector Twelve. I've crash-landed on a strange planet. The impact must have awoken me from hypersleep."

Buzz bounced up and down on the squishy surface of the bed. "Terrain seems a bit unstable," he reported into his communicator. "No readout yet if the air is breathable." He glanced around. "And there seems to be no sign of intelligent life anywhere."

Woody poked his head in front of Buzz. "Hello?"

"HOOO-YAAAAAHH!" Buzz jumped back, arms raised in a defensive stance.

Woody threw up his hands like a holdup victim. "Whoa! Did I frighten you? Didn't mean to. Sorry." He slowly lowered his right hand and held it out to the stranger. "Howdy! My name is Woody, and this is Andy's room. That's all I wanted to say. And also, there has been a bit of a mix-up. This is my spot, see, the bed here—"

"Local law enforcement!" Buzz interrupted, nodding at Woody's badge. "It's about time you got here. I'm Buzz Lightyear, space ranger, Universe Protection Unit. My ship has crash-landed here by mistake."

"Yes, it is a mistake," Woody agreed, "because you see, the bed, here, is my spot."

But Buzz didn't seem to be listening. He strode away, scanning the terrain of what he thought was a strange new planet. Woody hurried to keep up.

"I need to repair my turboboosters," Buzz informed the sheriff. "Do you people still use fossil fuels? Or have you discovered crystallic fusion?"

Woody took off his cowboy hat and scratched his head. "Well, let's see. We've got double-A batteries—"

Suddenly, Buzz yanked Woody flat down on the bed. "Halt! Who goes there?" he cried. Andy's toys were peeking over the edge of the bed.

"Don't shoot!" Rex yelled out. "It's okay! Friends!"

Buzz cocked his head toward Woody. "Do you know these life-forms?"

"Yes," Woody replied. "They're Andy's toys."

Buzz seemed to relax. "All right, everyone. You're clear to come up." He stood and walked over to the toys. "I am Buzz Lightyear," he said boldly. "I come in peace."

Rex rushed up and grabbed his hand, pumping it up and down with enthusiasm. "Oh, I'm so glad you're not a dinosaur!"

"Why, thank you," Buzz said, a puzzled look on his face. "Thank you all for your kind welcome."

Rex stared at the panel of buttons on Buzz's space suit. "Say! What's that button do?"

"I'll show you." Buzz pressed the button. A clear, bold recorded voice cried out: *"Buzz Lightyear to the rescue!"*

"Ooooooh!" the toys murmured.

"Hey," said Slinky. "Woody's got something like that. His is a pull string, only—"

"Only it sounds like a car ran over it," Mr. Potato Head joked.

"Yeah, but not like this one," Hamm said with admiration. "This is a quality sound system. Probably all copper wiring, huh? So, where are you from? Singapore? Hong Kong?"

Buzz looked at the piggy bank, one eyebrow raised. "Well . . . no, actually, I'm stationed up in the Gamma Quadrant of Sector Four. As a member of the elite Universe Protection Unit of the Space Ranger Corps, I protect the galaxy from the threat of invasion by the evil Emperor Zurg, sworn enemy of the Galactic Alliance."

The toys stared at Buzz in silence.

"Oh, really?" Mr. Potato Head said finally. "I'm from Playskool."

Frowning, Woody glanced at Buzz's box. On one side he could see a drawing of Buzz Lightyear. Printed in a cartoon balloon coming out of his mouth was the exact speech Buzz had just given!

Woody snorted and walked over to Bo Peep. He crossed his arms and forced a casual smile. "You'd think they've never seen a new toy before."

"Well, sure." Bo Peep shrugged. "Look at him. He's got more gadgets than a Swiss Army knife!"

Andy's toys crowded around the newcomer as if he were a movie star. Slinky shyly poked a finger toward a large red button on Buzz's upper arm.

"Ah-ah-ah!" Buzz warned, shaking his index

finger like a fussy schoolteacher. "Please be careful. You don't want to be in the way when my laser goes off."

"A laser!" Mr. Potato Head exclaimed. He shot Woody a mischievous look. "How come *you* don't have a laser, Woody?"

"It's not a laser! It's a little lightbulb that blinks!" Woody was usually pretty easygoing, but all this fuss over Buzz was starting to bother him.

"Look, we're all very impressed with Andy's new toy—" Woody began.

"'Toy'?" Buzz exclaimed scornfully.

Woody nodded with a smug smile. "*T-O-Y.* Toy."

"Excuse me," Buzz said firmly. "I think the word you're searching for is *space ranger.*"

"The word I'm searching for I can't say because there are preschool toys present!" Woody yelled.

Mr. Potato Head chortled. "Gettin' kind of tense, aren't you, Sheriff?"

"Mr. Lightyear?" Rex asked shyly. "What does a space ranger actually do?"

Woody rolled his eyes. "He's not a space ranger! He doesn't fight evil or shoot lasers or fly—"

"Excuse me." Buzz calmly pressed a button on his chest. An outrageous pair of high-tech wings sprang open on the back of his space suit. The other toys gasped in awe.

"Oh, what? What?" Woody couldn't believe how gullible his friends were. He grabbed hold of one of Buzz's wings. "These are plastic. He can't fly!"

Buzz raised his chin proudly. "They are a terillium-carbonic alloy, and I *can* fly."

Woody shook his head. "No, you can't."

"*Yes*, I can."

"You can't."

"Can."

"Can't! Can't! *Can't!*"

Buzz's eyes flashed angrily. "I tell you, I could fly around this room with my eyes closed!"

"Okay, then," Woody challenged the new-comer. "Prove it!"

"All right, then, I will!" Buzz strode toward the edge of Andy's bed. "Stand back, everyone!" he warned. "To infinity . . . and beyond!" He raised his arms and leaped off the bed. Woody grinned and waited for the *crunch!*

Boing! Boing? Woody dashed to the edge and looked down. Then he looked up. He couldn't believe it! Buzz had landed on a big rubber ball. He bounced. Then he plunged back down and landed on a toy race car. He went zooming down the track. He swooshed through a show-stopping loop-the-loop. He flew out of the car and into the air. His space suit hooked on to a mobile that swung him around and around, faster and faster.

Then, as his momentum grew, he hurtled off, flipped into the air, and landed squarely on the bed—right in front of Woody's nose.

"Can!"

The other toys began to clap and cheer

excitedly. Woody couldn't believe they actually thought Buzz had been flying.

"Wow!" Rex crooned. "You flew magnificently!"

Bo Peep winked. "I found my moving buddy!"

Buzz smiled modestly. "Why, thank you. Thank you all."

"That wasn't flying!" Woody exclaimed. "That was falling with style." He folded his arms and frowned. "In a couple of days, everything will be just the way it was," he said to himself. "They'll see. I'm still Andy's favorite toy."

Chapter

The next morning, Woody woke up stiff and sore. Darkness surrounded him. For a moment he couldn't remember where he was.

Then it all came back to him. Andy's room—which had been decorated with cowboy posters and drawings, even a cowboy bedspread, for as long as Woody could remember—was now full of space ranger decorations. Andy had new space ranger pajamas to replace his old cowboy pajamas. He clearly had a new favorite toy—Buzz. Even the other toys seemed to like Buzz better than Woody!

But worst of all, Andy had chosen Buzz over Woody at bedtime, which meant that Buzz got to sleep tucked under the covers next to Andy, while Woody had to do something he had never done before: sleep in the toy chest. He'd always slept in Andy's bed before Buzz came along!

Woody pushed up the lid of the toy chest and peeked out. All clear. He took a deep breath of fresh air. When he reached up to adjust his hat, he discovered it was missing.

A rubber shark popped up from the chest behind him, wearing Woody's hat.

"Look! I'm Woody! Howdy, howdy, howdy!" the shark shouted.

"Give me that!" Woody grabbed his hat and jammed it onto his head. He leaped out of the toy chest and slammed the lid.

Across the room, Buzz was already up, surrounded by adoring fans. No wonder he looked so good—he had slept in Andy's bed!

"It looks as though I've been accepted into your culture," Buzz told Rex and Slinky. Buzz raised his foot so they could see the sole of his shiny white space boot. The name ANDY was neatly printed in bold letters with a permanent marker. "Your chief, Andy, inscribed his name on me."

Woody gulped. He bent over and looked at the bottom of his worn, dusty cowboy boot. ANDY was written there, too, but in a childish scrawl. And the letters had begun to fade.

"Don't let it get to you, Woody," a gentle voice said. Woody quickly dropped his foot and looked up.

Bo Peep was smiling at him—something that usually made his heart do cartwheels. But today her smile looked different somehow. Today it was tinged with pity.

"Uh," Woody said, smiling back and trying to act nonchalant, "what do you mean? Who?"

"I know Andy's excited about Buzz," Bo Peep said. "But you know he'll always have a special place for you."

"Yeah," Mr. Potato Head cracked as he sauntered past. "Like the attic."

"All right! That's it!" Woody growled. He'd had enough of being pushed around and shoved aside. It was time to deal with this trespasser head-on.

Buzz Lightyear had his cardboard box "spaceship" up on blocks. He lay on a skateboard, then rolled himself under the box to do repairs. Snake and Robot hovered nearby, eager to be of service to their new hero.

But Woody stepped between them and pulled Buzz out from under the box. He glared into the surprised spaceman's face. "Listen, Lightsnack. You stay away from Andy. He's mine, and no one is taking him away from me."

"What *are* you talking about?" Buzz shook his head impatiently, then rolled himself back under the spaceship box.

Woody hauled him out again. "And another thing. Stop with this 'spaceman' thing. It's getting on my nerves."

Buzz sighed irritably and stood up. "Are you

saying you want to lodge a complaint with Star Command?"

"Okay, so you want to do it the hard way, huh?" replied Woody.

"Don't even think about it, cowboy," said Buzz.

"Oh, yeah, tough guy?" Woody shot back.

Woody poked Buzz in the chest—and accidentally jabbed a green button. Buzz's helmet whooshed open.

"AAGGGHHH!" Buzz clutched his throat, gasping for air. He dropped to his knees, then toppled onto his side, writhing on the ground and holding his breath. The robot and Slinky looked at each other nervously. Woody just rolled his eyes.

Finally, Buzz was forced to suck in a huge rasping breath. He waited a moment. He blinked. He sniffed. Then he exhaled. Nothing happened.

Buzz seemed stunned. "The air isn't toxic!" he exclaimed.

Then he turned on Woody. "How dare you open a spaceman's helmet on an uncharted planet! My eyeballs could have been sucked from their sockets!" Glaring, he whooshed his helmet closed.

"You actually think you're *the* Buzz Lightyear?" Woody said. Buzz just sniffed, as if insulted. "Oh, all this time I thought it was an act!" Woody continued. He turned to the other toys, who were gathering around. "Hey, guys! Look!" he said sarcastically. "It's the *real* Buzz Lightyear!"

Buzz cleared his throat, then blinked a couple of times. "You're mocking me, aren't you?"

Woody guffawed. "Oh, no, no, no." Then, staring over Buzz's shoulder, he twisted his face in horror and said, "Buzz, look! An alien!"

Buzz whirled around. "Where?" Woody clutched his stomach and fell over with laughter.

Suddenly, a dog barked. Woody's laughter died in his throat. All the toys froze and looked at the bedroom window, through which a cackle floated in from outside.

"It's Sid!" Slinky whispered.

Rex looked frightened. "I thought he was at summer camp."

"They must have kicked him out early this year," Hamm grumbled.

Buzz watched, confused, as the toys crept toward the window.

"Who is it this time?" Mr. Potato Head asked.

Woody pulled himself up on the windowsill and shook his head. "I can't tell. Where's Lenny?"

A set of windup binoculars waddled over. Woody picked up the toy and looked through him to survey the scene.

A boy was playing in his junk-filled backyard. He wore a torn black T-shirt emblazoned with a skull and crossbones. His mangy dog was digging holes.

This boy was not like Andy. There was something mean about him. Something cruel. He was taunting a miserable-looking toy soldier as he strapped a huge M-80 firecracker onto the soldier's back with masking tape. The boy laughed as he lit the fuse.

"Oh, no," Woody moaned, "it's a Combat Carl."

Buzz broke through the crowd and made his way to the windowsill. "What's going on?"

"Nothing that concerns you spacemen," Woody said. "Just us *toys*."

"I'd better take a look anyway." Buzz snatched Lenny from Woody's hands and glanced around. Then his mouth fell open. "Why is that soldier strapped to an explosive device?"

Woody steered the binoculars till Buzz could see the boy. "*That's* why—Sid."

"You mean that happy child?" asked Buzz.

"That ain't no happy child," Mr. Potato Head snapped.

"He tortures toys," Rex said, "just for fun."

"Well, then, we've got to do something." Buzz stepped onto the window ledge.

"What are you doing?" Bo Peep exclaimed, grabbing his arm. "Get down from there!"

Buzz pulled away. "I'm going to teach that boy a lesson!"

"Yeah, sure," Woody mocked. "You go ahead. Melt him with your scary laser." He poked at Buzz's control panel, making it beep.

"Be careful with that!" Buzz said. "It's extremely dangerous."

Lenny saw that the fuse on Sid's explosive had almost burned down. "Hit the dirt!" he cried. The toys scattered, shrieking.

BOOM! BA-BA-BOOM! Woody and Buzz were thrown to the floor. They could hear bits and pieces of toy shrapnel pelting the side of Andy's house. Then they heard Sid laughing.

"Yes! He's gone! He's history!" shouted Sid from below.

Slowly, the toys rose from their hiding places and crept back to the window. Sid was jumping around the yard happily while Scud the dog barked and strained against the rope that kept him tethered to the back shed. All that was left of the Combat Carl was a smoky black smudge on the dirt. The toys cringed and turned away.

"I could have stopped him," Buzz said quietly.

"Buzz, I would love to see you try," Woody replied. "Of course, I'd love to see you as a crater."

But it was Bo Peep who spoke for them all. "The sooner we move, the better."

Chapter

A few days later, Andy and his mom decided to take a break from packing to go to Andy's favorite restaurant, Pizza Planet. Mrs. Davis told Andy that he could bring a toy. But only one.

Woody wanted to be that toy. He sneaked a peek at Buzz, who was standing a few paces away on Andy's desk. Then he grabbed a Magic 8 Ball and, shaking it, whispered, "Will Andy pick me?" He turned the 8 Ball over to see its prediction: DON'T COUNT ON IT.

Woody threw the 8 Ball down in disgust. It rolled across the desk and fell behind it with a loud thump. Woody peered into the narrow space between the desk and the wall. It was dark and deep and laced with cobwebs. The

8 Ball was wedged near the bottom. Woody noticed that the space was just big enough to fit a toy. He smiled to himself as an idea took shape.

Woody looked across the desk at Buzz. Then he looked over at Andy's radio-controlled race car, RC, who was parked at the other end of the desk. His nose was pointed directly at the spaceman. "Oh, Buzz! Buzz Lightyear!" Woody called, opening his eyes wide in mock alarm and running toward the space ranger. "Thank goodness! We've got trouble."

"Trouble? Where?"

Woody led him to the edge of the desk. "Down there. A helpless toy is *trapped*, Buzz!"

Buzz stared into the shadowy ravine. "I don't see anything."

"Oh, he's there," Woody assured him. "Just keep looking." Smothering a snicker, Woody backed up and grabbed the remote control, then flipped a switch. The car's headlight eyes flicked open. The motor hummed. Woody squeezed the remote. The car zoomed forward.

Buzz spun around. With a gasp, he leaped out of the way, and the car struck a bulletin board on the wall. The bulletin board fell and knocked a globe on Andy's desk off its stand, sending it rolling toward Buzz. He dashed across the desk, then fell, but he managed to roll out of the globe's way, onto the windowsill. As he regained his balance and got to his feet, the globe struck Andy's folding-arm desk lamp. The lamp swung around in a wide arc—and knocked Buzz right out the open window.

"Buzz!" Rex shrieked.

"Buzz!" Woody shouted. He couldn't believe the chaos he had caused.

Startled, many of the toys rushed toward the window. They hadn't seen what had happened. Woody crouched on the ledge on his hands and knees, staring down into the yard. There was no sign of Buzz anywhere.

"I don't see him in the driveway." Slinky

sounded worried. "I think he bounced into Sid's yard." Woody gulped and backed away from the window. Over on the desk, RC began to whirr.

"What is it, boy?" Rex asked.

"Whirrrr! Whirrrr! Whirrrr!"

Mr. Potato Head nodded knowingly. "He's saying that this was no accident."

"What do you mean?" Bo Peep asked.

"I mean Humpty Dumpty was pushed"—he glared at the sheriff—"by Woody!"

"Wait a minute," Woody said. "You don't think I meant to knock Buzz out the window, do you? Potato Head?"

"That's *Mr.* Potato Head to you—you back-stabbing murderer!"

"It was an accident!" Woody exclaimed. "Come on, guys. You gotta believe me."

Mr. Potato Head circled Woody like a prosecutor in a court of law. "Couldn't handle Buzz cutting in on your playtime, could you, Woody? Didn't want to face the fact that Buzz just might be Andy's new favorite toy. So you got rid of him.

Well, what if Andy starts playing with me more, Woody, huh? You gonna knock me out the window, too?"

Hamm stepped up beside Mr. Potato Head. "I don't think we should give him the chance."

Sarge quickly shoved the lid off the Bucket o' Soldiers. "There he is, men! Get him!" The soldiers jumped onto Woody's chest, knocking him off balance.

"Let's string him up by his pull string!" Mr. Potato Head shouted, leading a charge against the cowboy.

Suddenly, they heard Andy just outside the door. "Okay, Mom, be right down. I've got to get Buzz."

The startled toys dropped Woody and ran to their regular places. Andy came in and dashed to his desk. Then he stopped, puzzled. He looked around. He got down on his knees and searched the floor.

"Andy!" Mrs. Davis shouted. "I'm heading out the door!"

"But, Mom, I can't find Buzz!"

"Well, honey, just grab some other toy. Now, come on!"

"Okay. . . ." Disappointed, Andy looked around. He spotted Woody lying on the desktop. With a sigh, he grabbed the cowboy by the legs and hurried out.

Andy jumped down the front steps, then crossed to the driveway. As he passed the neatly trimmed bushes that lined the front of his house, a small plastic face poked out between some branches. It was Buzz Lightyear. And his temper was raging like a solar storm.

But Andy didn't see him. "I couldn't find my Buzz," he complained as he climbed into the van. "I know I left him right there."

Mrs. Davis buckled Molly into her car seat, then hopped in behind the steering wheel. "Honey, I'm sure he's around. You'll find him." She started the engine.

As the van rumbled to life, Buzz came out of the bushes and ran toward it. He leaped with all his strength—and grabbed on to the rear bumper just as the van pulled away.

"Can I help pump the gas?" Andy leaned forward in his seat and smiled at his mom. They had just pulled into a gas station.

"Sure," Mrs. Davis said. "I'll even let you drive."

"Yeah?" Andy asked, amazed.

"Yeah—when you're sixteen!"

"Funny, Mom."

Grinning, Mrs. Davis stepped down from the van. Andy slid open the side door and hopped out to help his mom.

Lying on the backseat by himself, Woody was miserable. Sure, Andy had brought him along—but he would rather have brought Buzz. Even worse, Woody's friends—the toys in Andy's room who had once admired him—now hated his guts. "How am I gonna convince those guys it was an accident?" Woody said sadly. As he gazed up through the open sunroof, something suddenly appeared in the small square.

"Buzz!"

Buzz leaped down onto the backseat. He was covered in mud. Bits of leaves and twigs stuck to his space suit. And he looked furious! But Woody was too overjoyed to notice.

"Buzz! You're alive! This is great! Oh, I'm saved! I'm saved! Andy will find you here, he'll take us back to the room, and then you can tell everyone that this was all just a big mistake. Huh?"

Buzz didn't say a word. He just glared.

"Right? Buddy?" Woody repeated nervously.

"I just want you to know," Buzz said calmly, "that even though you tried to terminate me, revenge is not an idea we promote on my planet."

Woody smiled. "Oh, that's good."

"But we're not on my planet, are we?"

And with that, Buzz lunged at him. Wrestling and scuffling, the two toys rolled off the seat, then tumbled out the open door of the van. The asphalt was hard and rough, and gas fumes filled Woody's nostrils as he and Buzz rolled beneath the vehicle.

Buzz landed a punch that sent Woody's head spinning around on his body. Woody countered by pummeling the spaceman's chest with both fists. Buzz's controls beeped and flashed. His helmet whooshed open and closed.

SLAM! Woody and Buzz froze.

Andy and his mom had jumped back into the van and slammed the doors. Through the open driver's-side window, Woody and Buzz could hear Mrs. Davis say cheerily, "Next stop—"

"Pizza Planet!" Andy finished for her. "Yeah!"

The engine roared to life. The van pulled away, its huge tires just inches shy of flattening Buzz and Woody into the asphalt. Lying in the open in a tangle of arms and legs, the two toys watched helplessly as the van's red taillights disappeared.

Chapter

"Andy?" Woody couldn't believe he'd been left behind. Desperately, he ran after the van, but he couldn't catch up.

"Doesn't he realize I'm not there?" Woody cried. "I'm *lost*! I'm a lost toy!"

Behind him, Buzz flipped open his wrist communicator. "Buzz Lightyear Mission Log. The local sheriff and I seem to be at a huge refueling station of some sort—"

"You!" Woody lunged furiously at Buzz.

But then a loud rumble shook the ground. High-beam headlights blinded the toys, and they froze. A giant tanker truck pulled into the station, and Buzz and Woody hit the asphalt.

The truck roared directly toward them,

stopping just a millimeter from Woody's nose. Glad to be alive, the two toys backed away from the monstrous wheels.

Buzz spoke into his wrist communicator: "According to my navi-computer—"

"Shut up!" Woody cried. "Just shut up!"

"Sheriff, this is no time to panic," Buzz said firmly.

"This is the perfect time to panic!" Woody snapped. "I'm lost, Andy is gone, they're going to move from their house in two days, and it's all your fault!"

"*My* fault?" Buzz shook his head. "If you hadn't pushed me out of the window in the first place—"

"Oh, yeah? Well, if you hadn't shown up in your stupid little cardboard spaceship and taken away everything that was important to me—"

"Don't talk to me about importance," Buzz growled. "Because of you, the security of this entire universe is in jeopardy."

"What? What are you talking about?"

Buzz gazed up into the starry night. He searched the constellations for a moment, then jabbed a finger toward a corner of the sky. "Right now, poised at the edge of the galaxy, Emperor Zurg has been secretly building a weapon with the destructive capacity to annihilate an entire planet! I alone have information that reveals this weapon's only weakness. And you, my friend, are responsible for delaying my rendezvous with Star Command."

Woody was speechless. He couldn't believe that this tiny toy space ranger—probably one of a million already sold—thought he was *real*. Woody's anger let loose, and he yelled into Buzz's face. "YOU ARE A TOY! You aren't the real Buzz Lightyear. You're an action figure! You are a child's *plaything*!"

Buzz shook his head. "You are a sad, strange little man, and you have my pity. Farewell."

"Oh, yeah?" Woody glared at Buzz's back as he strode off into the darkness. "Well, good riddance, ya loony!" He walked away in the opposite direction, muttering under his breath, "'Rendezvous with Star Command' . . ."

Ding! Ding! Woody glanced up as a truck pulled in near the station's door. His face lit up! A teenager went inside to ask directions. And on the side of his truck were two of the most beautiful words Woody had ever seen: PIZZA PLANET.

It was a pizza delivery truck! All Woody had to do was get on it. Sooner or later it would head back to the restaurant where the Davises were having dinner. With any luck, Andy and his mom would still be there!

Woody ran a few steps, then skidded to a stop. "Oh, no! I can't show my face in that room without Buzz." He scanned the lot. Buzz was at the other end, stalking away.

"Buzz!" Woody chased after him. "Come back!"

Buzz didn't even break stride. "Go away."

"No, Buzz, you've gotta come back!" Woody thought hard and fast. Any second now that delivery boy was going to drive the truck away. He and Buzz just had to be on it. Somehow he had to convince Buzz!

Woody kept his eyes on the truck and tried to think.

Wait! That sign on top of the truck's cab that had the words PIZZA PLANET painted on—it was a rocket ship! Woody snapped his fingers. "Buzz!" he shouted. "I found a spaceship!"

Seconds later, Woody and Buzz peeked out from behind a stack of oilcans on display near the truck. "Now, you're sure this space freighter will return to its port of origin once it jettisons its food supply?" asked Buzz.

"Uh-huh," Woody drawled. "And when we get there, we'll be able to find a way to transport you home."

"Well, then," Buzz said firmly, "let's climb aboard." He strode toward the driver's-side door.

"Wait, Buzz! Let's get in the back. No one will see us there."

"Negative," Buzz replied without a second of hesitation. "There are no restraining harnesses

Woody the cowboy is Andy's favorite toy.

Woody calls a meeting.

Rex and Slinky welcome Buzz to Andy's room.

Woody tries to show Buzz who's in charge.

The toys can't believe Buzz has fallen out the window!

Buzz becomes a Pizza Planet prize.

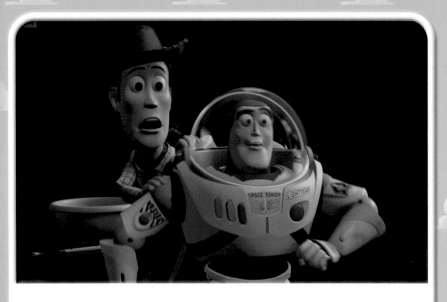

Buzz and Woody are desperate to escape Sid's room.

Woody asks the mutant toys for help.

The toys scare Sid.

Woody's plan works!

Scud chases Buzz and Woody.

Slinky tries to help.

Buzz, Woody, and RC are about to blast off.

The toys watch Buzz and Woody try to catch up.

Buzz and Woody fall—with style.

Andy's favorite toys are back where they belong.

in the cargo area. We'll be much safer in the cockpit."

Gracefully Buzz leaped into the air, grabbed the side mirror, and swung himself through the open window into the cab. Woody jumped up again and again, desperately trying to reach the mirror. Footsteps! The driver was coming!

Panicking, Woody ran around to the rear and scrambled up over the tailgate. After catching his breath, he moved forward to peer through the window into the cab. Buzz settled into the passenger seat and fastened his seat belt. Luckily, the driver couldn't see Buzz—he was hidden by a tall stack of pizza boxes. Woody shook his head.

The teenage driver hit the gas, screeching off into traffic. Woody, without a seat belt, slammed against the tailgate and fell into a crumpled pile. He looked up just in time to see a huge metal toolbox tumbling toward him. *BAM!* Everything went black.

After hurtling through the dark night for what seemed like hours, the pizza delivery truck finally squealed to a halt. Buzz waited till the driver went inside the restaurant. Then he scanned the terrain.

This was Pizza Planet, all right. Two armored sentries stood guard by the front door. Buzz didn't realize they were just animatronic robots. He thought they were real.

As two humans approached, the guards parted their crossed spears. *"You-are-clear-to-enter,"* the robots' recorded voices droned. *"Welcome-to-Pizza-Planet."*

Buzz turned around and pried open the sliding window that opened onto the truck bed. The back of the truck was empty, except for a large toolbox shoved up against the tailgate. "Sheriff!" Buzz hissed. A groggy Woody crawled out from behind the toolbox.

"There you are," Buzz said. "The entrance is heavily guarded. We need a way to get inside." Woody rose from the trash that was scattered about the back of the truck with a Mega-Gulp cup stuck on his head.

"Great idea, Woody!" said Buzz. "I like your thinking."

A few minutes later, the robot guards once again uncrossed their spears, allowing a family to enter Pizza Planet. At the same time, a burger box and a Mega-Gulp cup popped up next to a nearby trash can.

"Now!" cried Buzz from underneath the burger container. Hidden in the fast-food trash, Buzz and Woody rushed the door. "Quickly, Sheriff! The air lock is closing." Once inside, they sneaked between some video games and tossed off their disguises.

Buzz blinked in amazement. "What a space-port!" A carnival of sights and sounds filled the room. Pinball machines and video games pinged and flashed.

Woody scanned the mob of kids, looking for

one special face. Then he saw him—Andy! He was talking to his mom about a game called Black Hole while Molly giggled and waved in her stroller.

All we have to do, Woody reasoned, *is get into that stroller—and we're home free.* He began to inch his way forward, motioning for Buzz to follow.

But Buzz was forging his own path. "Now we need to find a ship that's headed for Sector Twelve."

Woody grabbed Buzz by the arm. "No, Buzz. This way. There's a special ship." Woody darted toward Molly's stroller, thinking that Buzz was right behind him.

But Buzz wasn't right behind him. He'd stopped to stare in wonder at what he thought was the most beautiful spaceship in the entire universe. In reality, it was a prize machine called the Rocket Ship Crane Game—the kind where a player inserted some money, then moved the claw inside to grab a prize and drop it into a slot.

And this machine looked like a spaceship. Buzz whistled and headed toward it.

Meanwhile, Woody was all ready to slip into Molly's stroller when he realized that Buzz wasn't with him. Woody spotted Buzz climbing up the crane game. "No! This cannot be happening to me!" Woody exclaimed as he stomped down the aisle to get Buzz.

By the time he caught up, Buzz had managed to slip inside the machine. Woody groaned as Buzz leaped into a pile of squeaking squeeze-toy aliens.

"A stranger!" one shouted.

"From the outside!" said another.

"Greetings! I am Buzz Lightyear! I come in peace."

Reluctantly, Woody climbed into the machine through the prize slot. He plopped down into the squeaky pile of aliens just in time to hear Buzz say, "This is an intergalactic emergency. I need to commandeer your vessel to Sector Twelve! Who's in charge here?"

The aliens pointed upward reverently. A mechanical claw dangled above them.

"The claw!" they murmured.

"The claw is our master," said one alien.

"The claw chooses who will go and who will stay," said another.

"This is ludicrous," Woody said to himself.

Suddenly, Woody heard a familiar but menacing laugh. He turned around and saw Sid heading straight for the crane game.

"Get down!" Woody shouted. He tackled Buzz, dragging them both under a layer of aliens.

"What's gotten into you, Sheriff?" Buzz exclaimed. Woody started to argue but was interrupted by the sound of Sid stuffing quarters into the coin slot. The machine began to hum. Sid yanked on the joystick. Slowly, the crane jerked around.

"The claw!" cried an alien. "It moves!"

Woody inched downward as the crane hovered directly above them. The jaws of the claw snapped open, then plunged into the pile. Woody closed his eyes. He felt the alien just above them rise.

"Gotcha!" Sid exclaimed.

"I have been chosen!" the little rubber creature cried joyfully. "Farewell, my friends. I go on to a better place."

But now Buzz lay exposed at the top of the pile of aliens. Before Woody could yank him farther down, Sid spotted the toy spaceman. "A Buzz Lightyear? No way!" he exclaimed.

Sid jammed more quarters in for another shot. The crane cranked up. Sid jerked on the joystick, steering the claw toward Buzz.

Woody searched for a way out. At the back of the machine, he spotted a small door. After a few tries, he managed to pry the door open. Woody grabbed Buzz, seizing him by the boots—just as the claw chomped down on his helmet.

"Yes!" Sid cried.

Woody pulled back on Buzz. But then some of

the aliens began to fight him, pushing the spaceman upward.

"Hey!" Woody cried. "What are you doing?"

"He has been chosen!" an alien explained.

"Do not fight the claw!" another warned.

Woody hung on to Buzz's leg and felt himself being dragged into the air.

"All right!" Sid cried at the sight of Buzz and Woody. "Double prizes!" He skillfully maneuvered the claw toward the corner prize slot. The jaws flexed open.

Woody and Buzz tumbled down the slot—and into Sid's hot, grimy hands. Clutching his prizes, he hurried toward the exit.

"Let's go home and . . . play!" laughed Sid.

Chapter

As Sid leaped off his skateboard and headed up the front path to his house, Buzz peeked out of Sid's backpack.

"Sheriff," Buzz whispered to Woody, who was squeezed in next to him. "I can see your dwelling from here. You're almost home."

The squeaky alien Sid had won wriggled up between them. "Nirvana is coming! The mystic portal awaits!"

"You guys don't get it, do you?" Woody cried. "Once we go inside Sid's house, we won't be coming out."

Sid opened his front door to a barking Scud, who pounced at the backpack.

"Scud! Hey, boy! Sit!" said Sid, holding his

backpack in front of Scud. The dog obeyed with a growl.

"Good boy. Hey, I got something for you, boy."

Woody pressed himself down into the pack as Sid's hand plunged inside. *Squeak!* The alien toy was smiling as Sid yanked it out and placed it on the dog's snout.

"Ready, set, *now!*" Sid commanded. Scud flipped the alien up into the air, caught it in his mouth, and began to shake it back and forth ferociously. Buzz and Woody looked on in horror.

Sid shoved open the door and, without wiping his feet, stomped inside. "Hey, Hannah!" Sid's little sister stood in the front hall holding a worn-looking Janey Doll.

"Did I get my package in the mail?" Sid asked.

"I dunno," Hannah replied.

"What do you mean, you don't know?" demanded Sid.

"I don't know!" insisted Hannah.

Sid's eyes narrowed. "Oh, no, Hannah!

Look—Janey!" He snatched the doll from her hands. "She's sick! I'll have to perform one of my . . . operations!"

"No!" Hannah cried. "Don't touch her!"

Sid ran upstairs to his room and slammed the door in Hannah's face. He threw his backpack on the bed. Woody and Buzz peeked out. They watched, stunned, as Sid clamped the Janey Doll's head in a vise and began to "operate," grabbing various items from his makeshift workbench.

"Hannah?" Sid called when he was finished. He went to the door and flung it open. "Janey's all better now," he said to his worried-looking sister as he handed her the doll.

Hannah shrieked. Janey's head was gone, and in its place was the head of a plastic pterodactyl. "Mom!" Hannah screamed as she turned and ran.

Sid tossed the doll over his shoulder and chased after Hannah, trying to get to his mother first. "She's lying! Whatever she says, it's not true!" he cried as the door slammed shut behind him.

Buzz and Woody took in their surroundings. Sid's room was a disaster. There were posters of heavy-metal bands on the wall. The bed was unmade. Dirty clothes, discarded toy parts, and power tools littered the floor. Shadows lurked in every corner.

"We are gonna die," Woody moaned as he climbed out of the backpack, ran across the bed, and dived onto the doorknob. "I'm outta here!"

But the door was locked from the outside. Woody dropped to the floor. "There's got to be another way out." A strange rustling sound made him turn.

A plastic yo-yo rolled quietly across the floor, then fell on its side. Woody grabbed a pencil from the floor and held it like a weapon. A shadow floated past him. He whirled around but saw nothing.

"Buzz? Was that you?" Woody called in fear, dropping the pencil and snatching a nearby flashlight. He heard a noise from under Sid's bed. He turned on the flashlight and pointed it in the direction of the noise.

A face inched into the light, and Woody sighed in relief. It was only the head of a baby doll. "Hi there, little fella! Come out here. Do you know a way out of here?" The head moved forward out of the shadows.

Woody choked down a scream. The doll head was mounted on a spider-like body made from the parts of an Erector set. With a soft whirring sound, the baby-faced creature stretched its metal legs until it towered over the astonished cowboy.

Woody glanced nervously around the room. Other strange mutilated toys darted out from the shadows. There were a toy fishing pole with fashion-doll legs, a skateboard with a soldier's torso screwed onto its front end, a jack-in-the-box with a rubber hand for a head, and many other frightening creations.

Woody clambered back up onto the bed and cowered behind Buzz. They watched as the

mutants dragged all the Janey Doll and pterodactyl parts into the shadows.

Woody's guts lurched. "They're cannibals!"
He leaped into the backpack, with Buzz right behind him.

Buzz punched a button on his chest. "May-
day! Come in, Star Command. Send reinforce-
ments!" He paused. "Star Command, do you
copy?"

No response. Buzz sighed and adjusted a
knob on his suit. *Blip!* "I've just set my laser from
stun to kill," he told Woody.

"Great," Woody muttered. "If anyone attacks
us, we can blink 'em to death."

Next door, Rex pointed a flashlight through
Andy's bedroom window into the dark bushes
below. Bo Peep, Mr. Potato Head, and the other
toys looked on, hoping to spot Buzz.

Suddenly, they heard a car approaching. Rex
turned off the flashlight, and they watched as

the Davises' van pulled into the driveway. As Mrs. Davis hopped out to unbuckle Molly from her car seat, Andy climbed out of the van and began looking under the backseat. Then he searched the front seats, too.

"He's not here, Mom. Woody's gone!"

Upstairs, the toys looked at one another.

"Woody's gone?" Bo Peep gasped.

"The weasel ran away!" Hamm cried.

"I told you he was guilty," Mr. Potato Head bragged.

One by one, the toys moved away from the window, until only Slinky and Bo Peep were left.

"Oh, Slink, I hope he's okay," said Bo Peep.

"A survivor!" Sid's voice rang out the following morning. He snatched Woody up and sent him flying across the room. Woody landed on the floor, hard.

"I can see your will is strong," said Sid. "Well, we have ways of making you talk."

Sid opened the blinds. Bright sunlight slanted sharply through the windowpane. He pulled out a magnifying glass and slowly, carefully, directed a beam of sunlight onto Woody's face. After a few moments, a tiny wisp of smoke curled up from Woody's forehead as it began to burn.

"Sid!" his mother shouted from downstairs. "Your Pop-Tarts are ready!"

"All right!" Sid hollered back. He threw down the magnifying glass and ran out of the room. As soon as he was gone, Woody let out a howl. Fanning his face, he dashed toward a nearby bowl of half-eaten cereal and dunked his head into the leftover milk.

Buzz ran over and pulled Woody out, searching his face for damage. Then he grinned and whacked Woody on the back. "I'm proud of you, Sheriff. A lesser man would have talked under such torture."

Woody sighed and looked at his reflection in the rounded side of the cereal spoon. He rubbed at a black smudge on his forehead. "I sure hope this isn't permanent."

Then he noticed something else reflected in the spoon and grabbed Buzz's arm. "The door! It's open! We're free!"

"Woody, we don't know what's out there!" Buzz warned.

Woody and Buzz ran for the door, but Baby-head, the half-doll, half-spider creation, suddenly crawled into Woody's path, followed by several other mutilated toys.

"They're gonna eat us, Buzz. Do something, quick!"

"Shield your eyes!" Buzz cried. He fired his laser at the mutants. *Beep! Beep!* Nothing happened.

"You're a toy!" Woody shrieked. "Use your karate-chop action!" He grabbed Buzz and began to push a large button on his back. The spaceman's arm chopped up and down involuntarily.

"Hey! How are you doing that?" Buzz cried. "Stop that!"

But Woody ignored him. He held Buzz in front of him like a shield and backed toward the door as the arm chopped up and down. "Back!" he shouted at the mutants.

"Sorry, guys," Woody said when he reached the door, "but dinner's canceled!" He quickly let go of Buzz and ran. "There's no place like home. . . . There's no place like home . . . ," he murmured as he flew down the hallway.

He rushed down the staircase . . . but stopped at the landing with a gasp. Scud blocked his way. The dog was sprawled out asleep, snoring loudly. Slowly, one step at a time, Woody backed up. Then someone grabbed him and pulled him down the hall.

"Another stunt like that, cowboy, and you're going to get us killed," Buzz scolded.

"Don't tell me what to do!" replied Woody.

"Shhhhhh!" said Buzz.

Buzz darted over to the stairwell. After checking to make sure that Scud was still asleep, he motioned for Woody to follow him down the hall. Woody crawled on hands and knees across the floor toward Buzz. But when he stood up, the ring on his pull string snagged on the railing. As both toys began to creep down the hallway, the string was stretched tighter and tighter, until—

Snap! The ring slipped off the railing and flew toward Woody, releasing the sound of one of his recorded messages down the hallway: *"YEEEEEEEE-HAAAAAAAAAA!"*

Buzz and Woody jumped in surprise. Across the hall, Scud woke up.

"Giddyup, partner!" Woody's voice box talked on. *"We got to get this wagon train a-movin'!"* Scud started up the stairs with a growl.

"Split up!" Buzz ordered as he dived through an open doorway.

Woody flung himself through a different door, nearby. It led to a junk-stuffed closet. As he slammed the door behind him, an unsteady tower of clutter crashed to the floor.

Scud prowled back and forth, growling and

sniffing around the crack beneath the door. Then he turned and started to enter the TV room, where Buzz was hiding. Suddenly, Sid's dad, who lay dozing in front of the television, let out a loud snore. Scud retreated with a disappointed growl, heading back downstairs. Buzz breathed a sigh of relief. He had begun to tiptoe into the hall when a voice boomed:

"Calling Buzz Lightyear! Come in, Buzz Lightyear! This is Star Command!"

"Star Command!" Buzz cried. He quickly flipped open his wrist communicator. He started to speak but then heard a child answer for him:

"Buzz Lightyear responding! Read you loud and clear!"

Buzz whirled around to see a television screen. An image of outer space faded into a shot of a boy playing happily in his back-yard . . . with a Buzz Lightyear toy. Confused, Buzz stepped closer.

"The world's greatest superhero," the an-nouncer said, *"now the world's greatest toy!"*

Buzz winced at the word *toy*. As the announcer's voice droned on, ordinary kids demonstrated each feature described. *"Buzz has it all: Locking wrist communicator! Karate-chop action! Pulsating laser light! Multiphrase voice simulator!"* One by one, Buzz compared the abilities touted on the screen to his own powers.

His mouth fell open as he heard the TV toy say, *"There's a secret mission in uncharted space!"* He pushed the button on the chest of his own space suit and heard: *"There's a secret mission in uncharted space!"* The same message—in exactly the same voice!

"And best of all," the announcer added, *"high-pressure space wings!"*

The Buzz Lightyear toy on television seemed to fly across an uncharted planet. The Buzz voice cried, *"To infinity . . . and beyond!"* Then a disclaimer flashed across the bottom of the screen: NOT A FLYING TOY.

"Not a flying toy," the announcer repeated quickly.

His mind reeling, Buzz staggered toward the door. He glanced at his wrist communicator and saw something he'd never noticed before. Tiny lettering was pressed into the plastic: MADE IN TAIWAN.

Woody's taunting words now echoed in Buzz's mind: *"You are a toy! You can't fly!"*

Suddenly, Buzz stood up straight. His eyes sparked with determination. This was all some kind of weird mistake. He'd show them he could fly. He'd show them all!

He climbed the banister and stood tall on the railing. He pressed the button that released his magnificent "high-pressure space wings" and held his arms out wide, aiming at an open window above the stairwell.

"To infinity . . . and beyond!" he shouted as he leaped off the banister . . . and fell toward the hard floor below. *CRUNCH!*

For a few seconds, Buzz didn't move. Then he slowly rolled over. Eyes open wide in shock, he saw that his left arm was completely broken off at the shoulder. For a moment he stared. Then he simply turned away and lay still, his eyes closed in despair.

A minute later, Sid's sister, Hannah, picked him up and took him to her room.

Chapter

Tangled in dusty Christmas lights, Woody crawled through the mountains of junk in the closet and finally tumbled out into the hall.

"Buzz?" he called out softly. "The coast is clear. Buzz, where are you?"

Buzz's voice echoed from down the hall: *"There's a secret mission in uncharted space. Let's go!"*

"Really?" Woody heard Hannah coo. "That is soooo interesting."

Woody crept toward the voices till he reached an open doorway. Hannah's bedroom. He peeked inside.

Hannah was having a tea party. Several headless dolls were seated around a tiny table. And

Buzz was propped up at the head of the table, dressed in a frilly apron and a stylish hat.

"Oh, no!" Woody thought hard and fast. Then he ran down the hall and cleared his throat. He tried to make his voice sound high and feminine—like Sid's mom's—as he called out loudly: "Hannah! Oh, Hannah!"

"Mom?" Hannah hurried out of the room. As soon as she disappeared down the stairs, Woody sprang to life and bolted into her bedroom. He saw that Buzz had fallen facedown on the table.

"Buzz! Are you okay?" He picked up Buzz's broken-off arm. "What happened to you?"

Buzz bolted upright with a glazed look in his eyes. "One minute you're defending the whole galaxy"—he grabbed his arm from Woody and pointed it at the headless dolls—"then suddenly you find yourself suckin' down Darjeeling with Marie Antoinette and her little sister!" The headless dolls turned and waved.

Woody choked back a feeling of disgust and

helped Buzz to his feet. "I think you've had enough tea for today. Let's get you out of here."

Buzz grabbed Woody by the collar. "Don't you get it?" he shrieked, laughing hysterically.

Woody shook the spaced-out spaceman by the shoulders. "Snap out of it, Buzz!" He pressed the button to pop open Buzz's helmet and slapped him just hard enough to startle him. Then he politely closed the helmet.

Buzz seemed to regain his composure. He shook his head as he and Woody walked out into the hall. "I'm sorry," he said with a sigh. "You're right. I'm just a little depressed, that's all." Suddenly, Buzz dropped to his knees on the hardwood floor. "Oh, I'm a sham!" he wailed.

"Shhh!" Woody hissed nervously. "Quiet, Buzz!"

"Look at me," Buzz ranted on. "I can't even fly out of a window."

Woody stopped. He looked down the hallway. He could see through Sid's open window—right into Andy's bedroom across the way. "Out the window . . . ," he mumbled, thinking. "Buzz, you're a genius!" He grabbed the strand of Christmas lights and dragged Buzz toward Sid's room.

In Andy's room, Hamm and Mr. Potato Head were playing Battleship when they suddenly heard, "Hey, guys! Guys! Hey!" coming from the house next door.

Mr. Potato Head got up and wobbled toward the window. "Son of a building block! It's Woody!"

Hamm stared in shock. "He's in the psycho's bedroom!"

Bo Peep, Slinky, and Rex flocked to the window. "Woody?" Bo Peep said.

When he saw his friends, Woody waved like crazy. "Boy, am I glad to see you guys!"

"I knew you'd come back!" Slinky cried.

"What are you doing over there?" Bo Peep asked.

"It's a long story," Woody said. "I'll explain

later. Here! Catch this!" Woody tossed the string of lights toward Andy's window. Slinky grabbed the end.

"Good going, Slink!" Woody called. "Now, just tie it onto something."

"Wait!" Mr. Potato Head grabbed the lights. "I got a better idea. How about we don't?"

"Hey!" Slinky said.

"Potato Head!" Bo Peep cried.

"Have you forgotten what he did to Buzz?" The toy shook his head in astonishment. "And now you want to let him back over here?"

Woody was stunned. "You got it all wrong, Potato Head. Buzz is fine! Buzz is right here. He's with me!" He turned his head, calling back into Sid's room. "Buzz, come over here and tell the nice toys that you're not dead."

But Buzz just sat on the floor, peeling the sticker off his wrist communicator.

Woody groaned. "Just a sec," he called over to his friends. "Buzz!" he cried. "Will you get up here and give me a hand?"

Buzz tossed Woody his broken arm, with the hand still attached.

"Ha, ha. That's very funny, Buzz." Woody glared at the toy, then exploded: "This is serious!"

"Woody?" Slinky hollered. "Where'd you go?"

"He's lying," Mr. Potato Head told the crowd. "Buzz ain't there."

Woody rushed back to the window. "Oh, hi, Buzz," he said, trying to act casual. He pretended he was talking to someone inside Sid's room, but just out of sight from the window. "Why don't you say hello to the guys over there?"

Woody held up Buzz's severed arm and waved it in front of the window, careful not to let the broken end show.

"Hey, look!" Rex said. "It's Buzz!"

Mr. Potato Head's eyes narrowed. "Wait just a minute," he said suspiciously. "What are you trying to pull?"

"Nothing!" Nervously, Woody threw both hands in the air and shrugged, revealing the broken end of Buzz's arm. The toys all screamed in horror.

"That is disgusting!" Hamm said.

"Murderer!" Mr. Potato Head cried.

Woody realized his mistake too late. "No, it's not what you think. I swear!"

"Save it for the jury!" Mr. Potato Head snapped. "I hope Sid pulls your voice box out, ya creep!" He flung the string of Christmas lights out the window. It banged against the side of Sid's house, tinkling as a few bulbs smashed.

"Don't leave!" Woody cried. "You've gotta help us, please! You don't know what it's like over here!"

One by one, the toys drifted away from the window. Only Slinky remained.

"Slink, please! Please listen to me!" Woody begged. But Slinky could no longer look Woody in the eye. With a whimper, he lowered the blinds.

"No!" Desperate, Woody screamed, "Come back. SLI-I-I-I-INKYYY!"

His voice was drowned out by the first rumblings of a thunderstorm.

Woody stood alone at the window, watching Andy's house. Then he heard a noise on the floor.

The mutant toys were attacking Buzz! Woody watched in terror as they converged on the space ranger.

Woody rushed to the rescue, still holding Buzz's broken arm. Suddenly, Babyhead turned and snatched Buzz's arm with his Erector-set pincers. Woody tried to yank it back, but he lost his grip and went flying across the room empty-handed. His stomach lurched as he watched the mutants swarm over Buzz's limp body.

"He is still alive. And you're not gonna get him, you monsters!" Woody shouted. He grabbed at the mutant toys, tossing them left and right as he tried to reach Buzz.

When Woody finally made it to the center of

the mob, the mutant toys unexpectedly moved back into the shadows. He found Buzz sitting up, a puzzled look on his face. He was rubbing his newly reattached arm.

Confused, Woody reached out and shook Buzz's arm. "Hey, they fixed you! But—but they're cannibals. We saw them eat those other toys."

Woody looked around the room. He watched as the mutant toys parted to reveal that the Janey Doll and the pterodactyl had been repaired, too. They all stared innocently at Woody.

"Uh . . . sorry," he said. "I thought that you were gonna . . . you know, eat my friend." Woody tried to apologize, but the mutants turned and scurried back into the dark shadows. He soon realized why: Sid was coming!

Woody grabbed Buzz and tried to drag him to safety. "Come on, get up!" But Buzz jerked his arm away and continued to stare at the floor.

"Fine!" Woody grunted. "Let Sid trash you. But don't blame me."

Woody left Buzz lying in the middle of the floor and ran to hide under a nearby milk crate, just as Sid opened the door and rushed in, carrying a big package.

"It came!" he shouted. "It finally came! The big one!"

He ripped open the package. Inside lay a large firecracker rocket with the words THE BIG ONE printed on its side. He looked around. "What am I gonna blow? Hey . . . where's that wimpy cowboy doll?"

He shoved some junk off his desk, looking for Woody. Sid spotted the milk crate and picked it up, but he didn't see Woody clinging to the inside. Sid suddenly heard the sound of a laser and looked down to see that he was stepping on Buzz.

"Yes! I've always wanted to put a spaceman into orbit," Sid said. He put the milk crate down on his desk, grabbed Buzz, and picked up his toolbox. He threw the toolbox on top of the crate and opened it. The impact caused Woody to fall from his hiding place. Woody watched as Sid pulled a roll of electrical tape from the toolbox and strapped Buzz onto the rocket. Sid stepped back with a snicker.

BA-ROOM! A huge thunderclap, followed by a flash of lightning, stopped Sid in his tracks. Thick raindrops began to pelt the windowpanes. "Aw, man!" exclaimed Sid. But then his frown turned into a grin. "Sid Phillips reporting," he said as if he were a TV reporter. "Launch of the shuttle has been delayed due to adverse weather conditions at the launch site. Tomorrow's forecast: sunny. Ha, ha, ha!"

He smacked Buzz down on the desktop, set his alarm clock, and placed it, ticking, right next to Buzz's ear. With a sinister smile he whispered to the spaceman, "Sweet dreams."

Next door, Mrs. Davis tucked Andy into bed and handed him his cowboy hat. He had been searching everywhere for his two missing toys.

"What if we leave them behind?" Andy asked.

Mrs. Davis smoothed Andy's hair back off his forehead. "Don't worry, honey. I'm sure we'll find Woody and Buzz before we leave tomorrow."

Andy sighed and shut his eyes. Once his mother turned out the light and left the room, a box on the floor marked ANDY'S TOYS began to shake from side to side.

"Will you quit moving around?" Mr. Potato Head complained.

"I'm sorry. It's just that I get so nervous before I travel," replied Rex.

"How did I get stuck with *you* as a moving buddy?" Mr. Potato Head retorted.

"Everyone else was picked," sighed Rex.

As the pair settled back down among the packing peanuts, Bo Peep peeked out of a nearby box and looked at the sleeping Andy.

"Oh, Woody, if only you could see how much Andy misses you," she said with a sigh.

Chapter

In Sid's bedroom, Woody struggled to free him-self from his milk-crate prison, but it wouldn't budge. Across the desktop, the once-proud Buzz Lightyear was still shamefully taped to the cheap rocket. "Psst! Hey, Buzz!" whispered Woody.

No response. Woody picked up a stray washer and tossed it at Buzz, trying to get his attention. *Clink!* The washer struck Buzz's helmet. Slowly, he looked over.

Woody waved wildly. "Hey! Get over here and see if you can get this toolbox off me!" Buzz just looked away.

"Oh, come on, Buzz. I can't do this without you. I need your help," pleaded Woody.

"I can't help," Buzz said flatly. "I can't help anyone."

"Why, sure you can, Buzz. You can get me out of here and then I'll get that rocket off you, and we'll make a break for Andy's house," said Woody.

"Andy's house. Sid's house." Buzz shrugged. "What's the difference?"

"Buzz, you've had a big fall. You must not be thinking clearly!" exclaimed Woody.

"No, Woody," Buzz responded. "For the first time, I *am* thinking clearly. You were right all along. I'm not a space ranger. I'm just a toy. A stupid, little, insignificant toy."

"Wait a minute," Woody said. "Being a toy is a lot better than being a space ranger."

"Yeah, right," Buzz said.

"No, it is!" Woody insisted. He pointed through the window toward Andy's room. "Look, over in that house is a kid who thinks you are the greatest, and it's not because you're a space ranger, pal, it's because you're a *toy*. You are *his* toy!"

Buzz looked down at himself, at his plastic parts and fake control panel. "But why would Andy want *me*?"

Woody sighed and shook his head. "Why would Andy want you? Look at you! You're a Buzz Lightyear! Any other toy would give up his moving parts just to be you. You've got wings, you glow in the dark, you talk, your helmet does that . . . that whoosh thing. You are a *cool* toy.

"As a matter of fact," he went on, "you're too cool. I mean—what chance does a toy like me have against a Buzz Lightyear action figure? All I can do is . . ." Woody pulled his own string.

"There's a snake in my boots!" his voice box chirped. Woody shook his head in disgust. "Why would Andy ever want to play with *me*, when he's got *you*?" He sighed. "I'm the one that should be strapped to that rocket."

Woody slumped against the milk crate, his back to Buzz. On the floor, Buzz raised his foot. He could still read ANDY through the dirt and scuff marks on the sole of his space boot. Buzz glanced back at Woody, a look of determination spreading across his face.

"Listen, Buzz, forget about me. You should get out of here while you can." When Buzz didn't respond, Woody turned around.

Buzz was gone.

Suddenly, the milk crate began to shake. Woody hung on and looked up. With the rocket still taped to his back, Buzz stood on top of the crate, trying to push the toolbox off.

"Buzz! What are you doing?" Woody asked. "I thought you were—"

"Come on, Sheriff," Buzz said, grunting. "There's a kid over in that house who needs us. Now let's get you out of this thing."

Together they began to push the milk crate. It started to budge, but it moved very slowly.

By now the sun was rising, warm and bright, drying up the night's rain. Suddenly, Buzz and

Woody heard the rumble of a vehicle pulling into Andy's driveway.

"Woody! It's the moving van!" exclaimed Buzz.

"We've got to get out of here—now!" cried Woody.

Buzz pressed back against the wall and pushed the toolbox with his feet. The toolbox began to move! With every shove, the milk crate inched out over the edge of the desk. When the gap was wide enough, Woody jumped through and landed on the floor below.

"Buzz! Hey, I'm out!" he called. But Buzz didn't hear. He kept pushing, until . . . *CRASH!* The toolbox and the milk crate fell off the desk and landed right on top of Woody.

Buzz glanced at Sid—miraculously, he was still snoring away—then ran to the edge of the desk. "Woody!" he whispered. "Are you all right?"

Woody crawled out from the rubble of tools, a little wobbly, and waved. "I'm fine. . . . I'm okay," he called up to Buzz.

BRIIIIIIIIINNNGG! The alarm clock rang.

Woody dropped back under the toolbox, and Buzz fell limp on the desk. As Sid sat up, his eyes brightened.

"Oh, yeah! Time for liftoff!" He threw back the covers, grabbed Buzz, and bolted from the room. The second Sid was gone, Woody leaped to catch the door before it closed. He pulled it open.

"*GRRRRRRRRR!*" There stood Scud! The dog pounced . . . but Woody slammed the door shut just in time.

"Okay, what do I do? Come on, Woody, think!" He looked around the room and discovered that the mutant toys had come out of hiding.

"Guys!" Woody exclaimed. The toys scattered like frightened mice.

"No! Wait! Listen!" Woody called. "There's a good toy down there and he's—he's going to be blown to bits in a few minutes all because of me. We gotta save him!" He paused and motioned with both arms for them to come closer. "But I need your help."

The toys stayed hidden. Woody noticed Baby-head timidly peeking out from under the bed.

"Please. He's my friend," Woody pleaded. "He's the only one I've got."

Babyhead crawled out of the corner and banged on the side of Sid's bedpost. Slowly, the rest of the mutant toys emerged from the shadows and gathered around Woody.

Woody knelt in the middle. "Thank you," he said to Babyhead. Then he turned toward the others. "I think I know what to do. We're going to have to break a few rules, but if it works, it'll help everybody."

In the backyard, Sid came out of a shed carrying a bunch of materials under his arm. He dropped them next to Buzz.

"Launchpad is being constructed!" he said with a menacing chuckle.

Meanwhile, back in Sid's bedroom, Woody studied a diagram of the Phillipses' house constructed out of stray dominoes and Scrabble pieces. He pointed to his makeshift map as he began to call out directions. "All right, listen up. I need Pump Boy here. Ducky here. Legs?" The toy fishing rod with fashion-doll legs strolled up.

"You're with Ducky." Woody jerked a thumb at a duck-head Pez dispenser with a baby-doll torso and a suction-cup base. "Roller Bob and I don't move till we get the signal. Clear?" The mutants all nodded.

"Okay, let's move!" commanded Woody. Ducky and Legs pulled the metal faceplate off a heating vent and disappeared inside.

Several other toys stacked up like a bizarre totem pole to reach the doorknob. Woody jumped onto Roller Bob, the skateboard with a soldier's head and arms attached to its front. "Wind the frog!" he shouted. A race car with baby arms began to wind up a little tin frog mounted on monster-truck wheels.

Scud was still barking outside Sid's door. The toys manned their positions. Their eyes were on

Woody, whose arm was raised. "Wait for the signal."

Meanwhile, Ducky and Legs had crawled through the heating ducts to the front of the house. Ducky tied the end of Legs's fishing line around his waist. They removed the porch-light socket. Then Legs lowered Ducky through the opening.

Dangling by the front door, Ducky began to swing back and forth. At last, he swung far enough to reach his target—the doorbell. *Dingdong!*

Back in Sid's room, Woody lowered his arm to signal the other toys. "Go!" The toys yanked open the door. The windup frog was let loose. The plastic amphibian zipped between Scud's legs and flew down the hallway. Barking madly, the dog chased it.

Out front, Ducky rang the bell again. "I'll get it!" the toys heard Hannah shout. She opened the front door, only to find that no one was there.

Behind Hannah, the windup frog zoomed

down the stairs with Scud in close pursuit. The frog hurtled off the last step, speeding between Hannah's legs and out the front door. Hannah spun around when she heard Scud chasing Wind-up Frog. Ducky dropped down and nabbed Wind-up Frog with his arms. Then Legs reeled them in.

Scud burst between Hannah's legs, knocking her down as he raced onto the porch. He stopped and looked around, barking crazily, then looked up at the frog disappearing into a hole in the porch ceiling. With a growl, he realized he'd been tricked. He tried to scoot back inside, but Hannah slammed the front door in his face. "Stupid dog," she muttered.

As Hannah stormed off, Roller Bob zipped into the kitchen with Woody and the other mutant toys clinging to his skateboard. "Lean back!" Woody shouted as they approached the doggie door. Roller Bob popped a wheelie, and they all flew through the small pet-door flap and crashed into the bushes outside.

The toys parted the bushes. In the side yard, they could see Buzz tied to a makeshift launch-pad. Sid was in the shed. Woody scurried toward his friend.

"Woody!" Buzz whispered. "Help me out of this thing!"

"Shhhhh!" Woody said. "It's okay, everything's under control." He grinned confidently, then fell limp on a patch of grass a few feet away.

"Woody!" Buzz cried. "What are you doing?"

Just then, Sid came out of the toolshed. Buzz froze. "Houston, all systems are go," Sid said, pretending to be doing a real space launch. "Requesting permission to launch— Hey!" He spotted the toy sheriff lying on the ground and picked him up. "How'd you get out here?" He looked around, confused, and then smiled. "Oh, well, you and I can have a cookout later." He stuck a kitchen match in Woody's empty holster and tossed him onto the barbecue grill.

"Houston, do we have permission to launch?" Sid spoke into the box of matches as if it were a microphone. "Roger. Permission granted. You are confirmed at T minus ten seconds." Sid struck a match. "Ten! Nine! Eight! . . ." He moved toward the fuse. But before he could light it, a voice rang out: *"Reach for the sky!"*

Sid froze. "Huh?" He whirled around. Woody was still lying stiffly on the grill, but sound kept coming from his voice box: *"This town ain't big enough for the two of us!"*

"What?" Sid said.

Sid walked over to Woody and picked him up. *"Somebody's poisoned the water hole!"* said Woody's voice box.

"It's busted," said Sid.

"Who are you callin' *busted*, Buster?" Sid stopped and stared at Woody, eyes wide.

"That's right. I'm talking to *you*, Sid Phillips," Woody continued. Sid shook the toy, checking the pull string.

"We don't like being blown up, Sid, or smashed, or ripped apart. . . ."

Sid gulped. "W-w-we?"

"That's right," Woody said. "Your toys."

At that, the mutant toys, along with all the broken toys in the yard, rose from their hiding places like creatures in a horror movie. Sid trembled with fear as the mutilated toys surrounded him.

"From now on, you must take good care of your toys," Woody continued. "Because if you don't, we'll find out, Sid. We toys can see"— Woody's head spun around a full 360 degrees— "everything."

As Sid stared in terror at Woody's head, the cowboy's rigid plastic features suddenly came to life. "So play nice," he warned, glaring sternly at the boy.

"AAAAAAAAAAGGGGGGGHHHHHHH!!!!" Sid dropped Woody as if he were on fire and bolted toward the house. At the door he bumped into Hannah. She was carrying a new doll, and she clutched it protectively.

"The toys are alive!" Sid yelled. He stared at Hannah's doll. Hannah cringed, but Sid just smiled weakly. "Nice toy!" he said nervously.

Hannah, sensing Sid's fear, thrust the doll in his face. He screamed. "What's wrong, Sid? Don't you want to play with Sally?" she taunted as she chased him upstairs.

Outside, Sid's broken, twisted toys gathered around Woody and cheered. Woody shook the toys' hands, if they had hands, and congratulated everyone.

"Nice work, fellas," Woody told them. "Good job. Coming out of the ground—what a touch! That was a stroke of genius."

"Woody!" The cowboy turned. Buzz was still tied to the launchpad. He held out a hand to his friend. "Thanks." Woody grinned and shook hands with the spaceman.

HONK! HONK! Through the fence that surrounded Sid's yard, they heard Mrs. Davis's voice. "Everybody say 'Bye, house!'" she told her children.

"Bye, house," Andy said sadly.

"Woody! The van!" Buzz cried.

Woody freed Buzz from the launchpad. Together the cowboy and the spaceman sprinted toward the fence. The slim cowboy easily slipped through. He ran ahead and climbed onto the rear bumper of the family van. But Buzz, with the big rocket still attached to his back, got stuck in the fence.

"Just go! I'll catch up!" Buzz shouted.

But Woody couldn't leave his friend. He jumped down from the bumper and ran back for Buzz. Woody pushed and tugged on Buzz until he finally popped through the fence. They raced down the driveway and out into the street, where they watched the Davises' van pull away.

Chapter

*H*OOOONK! Woody and Buzz turned around just in time to see the moving truck driving toward them. With a scream, they ducked. As soon as the truck passed, Buzz began to chase it. "Come on!" he called to Woody.

Back at Sid's house, Scud was lying on the porch, but he perked up at the sight of the two little action figures running down the street. He bared his teeth and growled.

Buzz ran closer to the truck, with Woody just a few steps behind him. A strap dangled off the back of the truck. Buzz leaped . . . and caught it! Grunting, he climbed onto the bumper. Then Woody lunged for the strap—and missed.

"You can do it, Woody!" Buzz called out.

Woody tried again. This time he caught hold of the strap. "I made it!" He began to clamber up to the bumper, but suddenly he heard a furious barking. Looking over his shoulder, Woody could see Scud racing after the truck—the dog was closing in fast!

"Aaaaaaah!" Woody yelled as Scud's jaws chomped on his leg. He kicked at the dog with his other foot. "Get away, you stupid dog! Down! Down!" Scud continued to tug, pulling Woody down to the end of the strap.

"Hold on, Woody!" Buzz cried.

"I can't do it!" Woody gasped. "Take care of Andy for me!"

"Noooooo!" Bravely, Buzz leaped onto Scud's snout and pulled on the dog's eyelids. Scud yelped and let go of Woody. Dog and spaceman were left behind as the truck continued forward.

Thinking quickly, the cowboy scrambled up the strap and onto the truck's bumper. He unlocked the back door. When the moving truck screeched to a halt at a red light, the door flew upward, with Woody dangling from the handle.

Inside the truck, he spotted what he was looking for: several boxes scrawled with the words ANDY'S TOYS. Woody jumped down and yanked one open. Mr. Potato Head, Rex, and some of the other toys squinted in the sudden burst of sunlight.

"Are we there already?" Rex asked.

"Woody!" Slinky cried. "How'd you—"

But Woody was busy rummaging through another box. "There you are!" He pulled out RC, along with the remote. Then he ran to the back of the van and kicked the toy car down into the street.

"He's at it again!" Rex wailed.

Woody turned on the remote and steered the car toward Buzz. Scud had shaken the space ranger off, and now Buzz was trapped under a parked car. When the toy car zoomed up, Buzz jumped on. Using the remote control, Woody then guided RC back toward the moving truck. As the red light turned green and the truck started forward, RC and Buzz were close behind. But so was Scud!

Meanwhile, the toys in the moving truck didn't understand what was happening. All they saw was Woody throwing RC out the back of the truck.

"Get him!" Mr. Potato Head shouted, leading a mob of angry toys out of the box.

Rocky the wrestler grabbed Woody and spun him overhead. Woody was still holding the remote control, and the toy car began to spin, too, matching Woody's movements. Luckily, it was perfect timing—RC and Buzz spun away from Scud just as he was about to chomp down on them.

Rocky threw Woody to the floor, and the car resumed its straight course toward the truck. Scud gave chase as Buzz and RC drove right into a busy intersection. The toys made it through, but a traffic jam trapped Scud among a jumble of cars.

In the truck, the mob of toys lifted Woody

up. "Toss him overboard!" Mr. Potato Head shouted.

"No, wait!" Woody pleaded. "You don't understand. Buzz is out there! We've gotta help him!"

But the toys didn't believe him. "So long, Woody!" Mr. Potato Head sneered as the toys threw Woody out the back of the truck.

Woody hit the ground hard. A horn blared as a car swerved to avoid running over him. Shaken, he tried to stand up just as Buzz and RC came barreling toward him. They scooped him up and kept driving.

"Thanks for the ride," Woody said, still holding the remote. "Now let's catch up to that truck!" He flipped a switch on the remote from ON to TURBO. The toy car roared toward the moving truck.

Lenny was watching the action out the back of the truck when he spotted Woody and Buzz chasing after them. "Guys! Woody's riding RC! And Buzz is with him!"

Bo Peep peered through Lenny's lenses. "It *is*

Buzz!" she said. "Woody was telling the truth!"

"What have we done?" cried Slinky.

"Rocky!" Bo Peep ordered. "The ramp!" The wrestler ran toward a lever and pulled, releasing a loading ramp mounted on the back of the truck.

"Hold on to my tail!" Slinky woofed. Mr. Potato Head and Rex grabbed on to his tail, and Slinky jumped onto the ramp and held out his paw to Woody.

As RC neared the moving truck, Woody handed the remote to Buzz and grabbed Slinky's paw.

"That a boy, Slink!" Mr. Potato Head cheered.

But suddenly, RC began to slow down and swerve. As the moving truck pulled ahead, Slinky's middle stretched out . . . and out.

"Woody!" shouted Slinky.

"Speed up!" Woody ordered Buzz.

"The batteries! They're running out!"

Slinky's spring was stretched as far as it could go. His paw slipped out of Woody's hand and he snapped back into the truck, scattering the toys like bowling pins.

RC coughed and choked, then sputtered to a stop. Woody and Buzz watched helplessly as the moving truck drove on without them. Buzz threw down the remote.

"Great!" Woody cried in frustration.

Buzz sighed, then jumped to his feet and grabbed the sheriff's sleeve. "Woody! The rocket!"

Woody stared at the rocket still taped to Buzz's back. "The match!" Woody shouted. Smiling, he pulled out the kitchen match Sid had stuck in his holster earlier. "Yes! Thank you, Sid!"

Woody rushed around to the rocket and struck the match. He was just about to light the fuse when a car whizzed over them. A gust of wind blew out the flame. Woody fell to his knees and pounded the street with his fists. "No, no, nooooooo!"

Unable to watch Woody's despair, Buzz bowed his head. Suddenly, the sunlight that was streaming through his helmet acted just like Sid's magnifying glass. A tiny white-hot dot shone on the back of Woody's hand.

Getting an idea, Woody jumped up, grabbed Buzz's helmet, and aligned it so that the pinpoint of concentrated sunlight hit the tip of the rocket's fuse. "Hold still, Buzz," he ordered. At last, the fuse lit.

"You did it!" Buzz cried. "Next stop—Andy!" Woody jumped back onto RC. Suddenly, he stopped smiling.

"Wait a minute," he said. "I just lit a rocket. Rockets explode!"

And at that moment, the rocket ignited, blasting Woody and Buzz down the street so fast that RC flew inches above the asphalt. Woody struggled to hang on.

Soon the moving truck came back into sight. The rocket was so strong that it began to lift Buzz, Woody, and RC off the ground. Woody managed to hang on—but not for long. He lost his grip, and the toys in the moving truck managed to scatter just as RC hurtled into the back of the truck. The rocket—along with Buzz and Woody—flew higher and higher into the sky.

"Ahhh!" Woody hollered. "This is the part where we blow up!"

"Not today!" Buzz shouted. He pressed a button on his chest and his toy wings sprang open, cutting the electrical tape and separating him from the rocket.

As the rocket exploded just above them, Woody covered his eyes and prepared to fall. But Buzz used his body like a glider, and suddenly he and Woody were soaring.

"Buzz! You're flying!" exclaimed Woody.

"This isn't flying," replied Buzz. "This is falling—with style!"

"Ha, ha!" Woody cheered. "To infinity . . . and beyond!"

With easy confidence, Buzz swooped under some power lines and drifted gracefully toward the moving truck. But then he flew over it.

"Uh, Buzz? We missed the truck!" shouted Woody.

"We're not aiming for the truck!" Buzz replied.

Buzz tilted a little to the left, spun them in a loop, then sailed down through the open sunroof of the Davises' van. Before anyone could notice, Buzz and Woody landed in an open box in the backseat—right next to Andy.

As Andy turned away from the window he had been looking out of, he discovered Buzz and Woody lying in the box, their faces arranged in the exact same smiles they'd worn the first day he had laid eyes on them.

"Hey!" Andy exclaimed. "Wow!"

"What is it?" his mom called from the front seat.

"Woody! Buzz!" Andy cried.

"Oh, great, you found them," Mrs. Davis said. "Where were they?"

"Here!" Andy replied. "In the car!"

Mrs. Davis chuckled and shook her head.

"See? What did I tell you? Right where you left them."

Andy hugged both toys. Tucked in his arms, Buzz and Woody exchanged knowing smiles.

Epilogue

A few months later, in Andy's new home . . .
A cheery wreath hung on the front door. Lights twinkled around the frosty picture window. Inside the warm and cozy house, Andy's family gathered around a beautifully decorated Christmas tree.

Though it was early in the morning, Andy was wide awake, poking and prodding the presents beneath the tree. "Which one can I open first?" he asked his mom.

"Let's let Molly open one," Mrs. Davis replied.

As Andy handed his sister a present, one of the bulbs on the Christmas tree moved a quarter of an inch, and a small Green Army Man peeked out at the Davis family with his tiny green binoculars. Behind him, several soldiers clung to silver tinsel as they climbed into the tree. Another soldier reached for a knob on the baby monitor that was wedged between some sturdy branches.

Upstairs in Andy's room, the receiving end of the baby monitor crackled with static.

"Frankincense—this is Myrrh," Sarge's voice announced. *"Come in, Frankincense."*

Buzz leaned forward from his spot on Andy's bed. Beside the monitor, Hamm called out, "Hey, heads up, everyone! It's showtime!" Andy's toys chattered excitedly as they gathered on the floor below.

"Whoa! It's time!" said Rex. The toys ran toward the monitor. Woody was about to follow when a shepherd's crook yanked him backward. Bo Peep smiled at the sheriff and pointed up to a shelf, where her sheep dangled sprigs of mistletoe above the two dolls' heads.

"Say," Woody began. "Isn't that mistletoe?" Bo Peep nodded. Then she flung her arms around Woody and dipped him backward for a big old-fashioned kiss.

The rest of the toys clustered below the monitor in anticipation. The fear they had felt the day of Andy's birthday party was long gone.

"Quiet, everyone!" Buzz called out. The toys settled down to listen to Sarge's report.

"Molly's first present is . . . Mrs. Potato Head. Repeat: Mrs. Potato Head."

Hamm laughed, slapping Mr. Potato Head on the back. "Way to go, Idaho!"

"Gee," Mr. Potato Head said. "I better shave." He whipped off his plastic mustache piece and grinned.

Woody climbed onto the bed and sat down beside Buzz. The spaceman nodded hello, then stifled a grin when he saw the lipstick smears all over Woody's face.

"Come in, Frankincense," came Sarge's voice again. *"Andy is now opening his first present—"*

Static made his voice difficult to understand. Buzz banged on the side of the monitor sharply.

"Buzz Lightyear," Woody said, tipping his cowboy hat back on his head. "You're not worried, are you?"

"Me? No, no, no, no," Buzz said. Then he looked up anxiously. "Are you?"

Woody slung his arm around his best friend's shoulders and chuckled. "Now, Buzz, what could Andy possibly get that is worse than you?"

Suddenly, Andy gave an excited shout from downstairs. Buzz and Woody stared at each other, their smiles dropping into openmouthed shock as they heard yapping coming through the monitor. *Bark-bark-bark!*

Oh, no! There was just one thing worse than a brand-new toy: a brand-new *puppy*!